The Shy Mala

Story by Liliana Stafford
Illustrations by Sophia Zielinski

Windy Hollow Books

This book would not have happened without the help and support of the Warlpiri people. A special thank you goes to the traditional owners of the mala story: Otto Sims, Maxine and Loyd Spencer, Tess Ross, James Marshall, Neville Poulson, Bessy Nakamara, Chris Poulson, Cowboy George Ryder and Harry Nelson. Thank you for welcoming me and giving us your permission to share this beautiful story with children everywhere.
Liliana Stafford
Sophia Zielinski (Nangala)

Thanks to Dr Ken Johnson, Desert Knowledge Australia, for his generous assistance, and to June Butcher, Kanyana Wildlife Sanctuary, for telling me the original story. L. S.

 Thank you to Arts WA for helping to fund my trip to the central desert. S.Z.

First published in 2006 by
Windy Hollow Books
PO Box 265, East Kew, Victoria 3102, Australia

National Library of Australia
Cataloguing-in-Publication entry:

For children.
ISBN 1 921136 93 6.

1. Marsupials - Juvenile fiction. I. Zielinski, Sophia.
II. Title.

A823.3

Editorial consultants Janine Drakeford and Amanda Curtin
Designed by Nuovo Group
Pre-Press by Hell Colour Australia
Printed in China by Everbest Printing Co Ltd.

Forward by Boori Pryor

If a story teller believes what they breathe then their voice will tell the truth. Rhyme and timing give a story its heartbeat.

I believe the heartbeat to this great country is through its stories. A steadfast base that has stood the test of time. Stories are woven from the landscape, a landscape that has been shaped by scorching sun and crying rain, that is only unforgiving if it is not being listened to by all things that live among its majestic sunsets.

Liliana Stafford and her daughter Sophia have taken the spirit of the, almost extinct, Mala from its Tanami Desert home and together they have woven it into a new tapestry; one that respectfully uses the threads of wisdom from some of this country's oldest people the Warlpiri.

Perhaps through the fabric of this new tapestry, others who have previously hesitated will find the courage to follow in the footsteps of *The Shy Mala* back to the gathering of stories that still breathe with the passage of time.

In the western desert north of Alice, Warla,
a tiny shy mala, sat under a bush.

What was that? Danger!

Foxes searched the low scrub.
Cats prowled the dry gullies.

Warla darted from her hideout and zigzagged
across the desert.

She was a night-time animal, but she had no choice:
she had to find another place to hide.

Still there was danger.

This was her land, but soon there would be few
of her kind left.

The Warlpiri people understood. The mala were
their story and their totem. They had to hang
on to the story for new generations.

It was secret, dreaming, "business".

The elders held a meeting
and spoke to the people. The people spoke
to the Rangers. They told of their fears.

Rangers came to the desert. They brought soft brown traps made of netting and placed them in the bushes.

Warla was hungry.
She smelt the bait in the trap. Clunk!

Warla cowered in the trap. The netting blocked out the worst of the coming daylight but it couldn't stop the fear. She became more and more stressed.

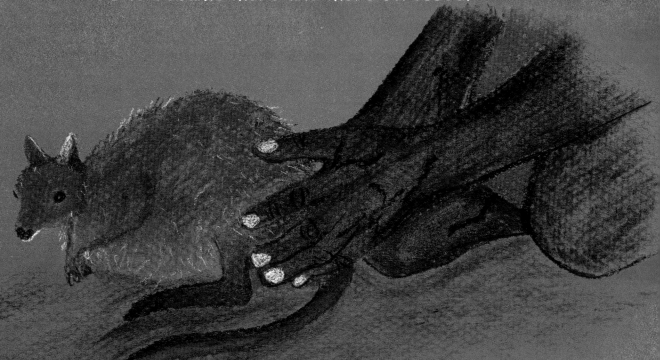

The Rangers came before dawn to rescue her.

Warla was taken to a fenced paddock where she would be safe from cats and foxes. Other mala were there.

The Warlpiri people knew she would not be staying long. They were sending her further away to a special enclosure called Barna Mia, in the Dryandra Woodland.

Once more Warla was caught and placed in a soft bag. Her fear grew. How could she know that the Warlpiri people and the Rangers wanted to help her?

The movement of the vehicle went on and on. Strange smells and sounds surrounded her. She could only wait and hope for it to end.

Finally the bag was opened and Warla was set
down on the ground under a bush.

Warla looked out.

The land where she knew this rock, that bush, was gone.

A different land lay before her, crowded with trees.

She hopped out of the bag and into the bushes.

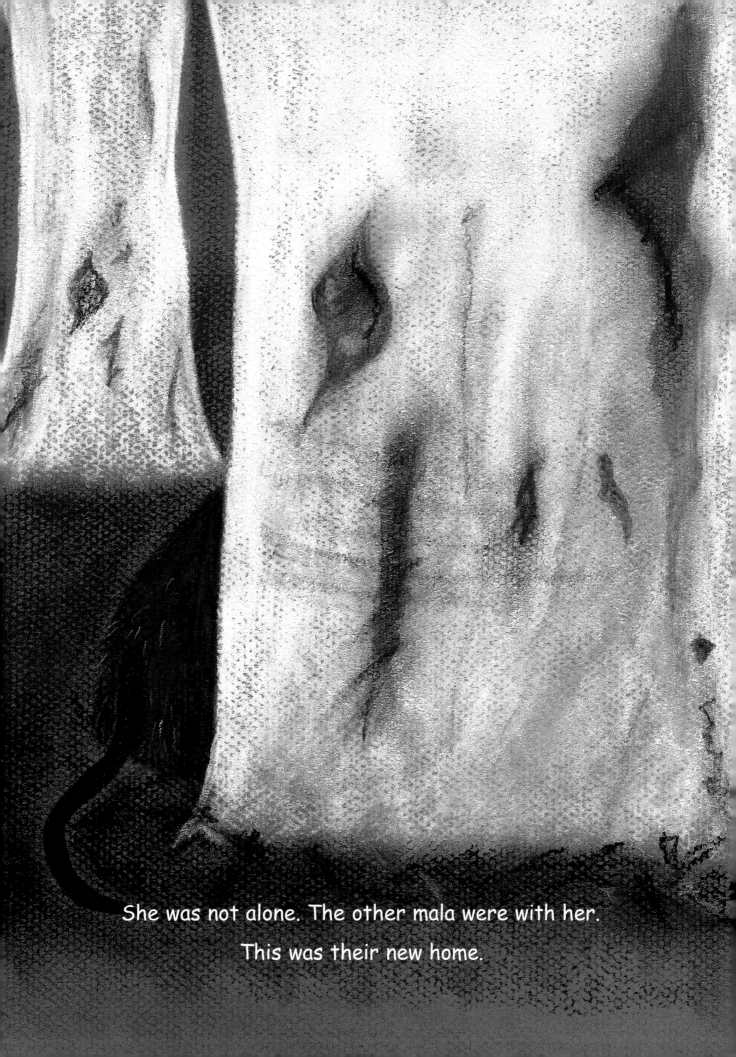

She was not alone. The other mala were with her.

This was their new home.

In the daytime Warla and the other mala stayed under bushes in small hollows scraped in the earth.

At night they came out to feed.

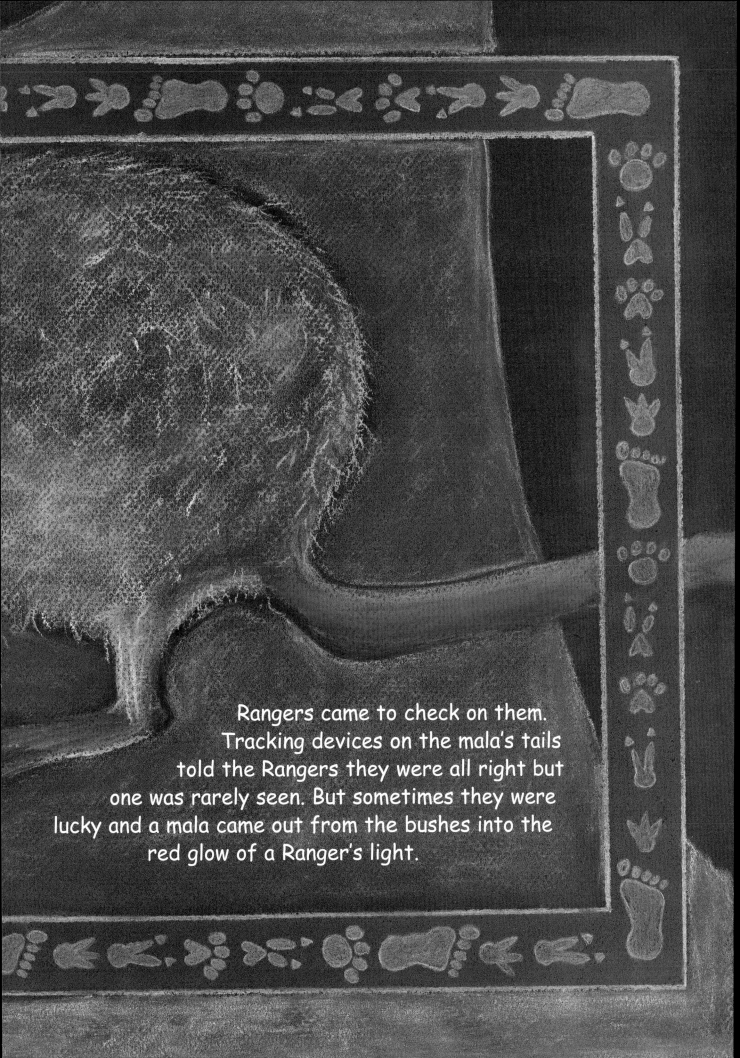

Rangers came to check on them.
Tracking devices on the mala's tails
told the Rangers they were all right but
one was rarely seen. But sometimes they were
lucky and a mala came out from the bushes into the
red glow of a Ranger's light.

Then one day the Warlpiri people
sent two of their elders.

They went all the way from Alice
to Western Australia.

In the middle of the day, with the sun high in the sky, they entered the Barna Mia enclosure. It was a big event. They were followed by reporters, photographers and Rangers.

The elders sat on the ground.
They began singing and playing sticks.

And a face poked out of one of the bushes,
then another, and another.

Warla was the first to come into the open.
The daylight was strong but she wasn't afraid.
She came right up to the elders.

The other mala followed.

Satisfied, the elders stood up to leave.

Their totem was safe.

Information about Mala

The mala, or rufous hare wallaby, weighing less than 1.4 kilograms, once inhabited the spinifex and hummock grasslands of the central deserts. It eats a variety of grasses, seeds, bulbs and sedges, plus some insects in the dry periods. The name "mala" is used by the Warlpiri people of the Tanami desert, north of Alice Springs, and many other Aboriginal language groups of the central region. The animal is culturally highly significant for the traditional families in this region, and mala law is celebrated in story, song and dance.

The story of the mala's journey from the desert to the Dryandra Woodland was first told to me in 1999 by June Butcher, who runs the Kanyana Wildlife Sanctuary in Gooseberry Hill, Perth, Western Australia.

The mala was once a common species but suffered a population collapse in the mid-twentieth century due to a poorly understood combination of drought, fire, predation from feral cats and foxes, and competition from introduced herbivores such as rabbits. To save the last remaining colony in the desert, a fenced paddock of about one square kilometre was built on Warlpiri Aboriginal land, where a thriving captive colony was established. Then in 1998 the Warlpiri people decided to send thirty mala to the Dryandra Woodland in the South West of Western Australia. Because the mala are extremely shy and sensitive to handling, they were caught in special soft traps made of nylon netting or shade cloth, called Bromilow traps.

Dryandra is a spectacular woodland of white-barked wandoo and powderbark, with thickets of rock sheoak. The mala are kept in a special enclosure called Barna Mia, with restricted access to people, and fenced from predators like cats and foxes. Other species in the enclosure are boodies, bilbies, marl and mernine.

The mala are now part of the Western Shield program run by CALM (Department of Conservation and Land Management). The program holds professional development weekends, field days and school workshops, at Barna Mia and throughout Western Australia, and is designed to increase understanding of native flora and fauna and to encourage active participation in helping to save endangered species.

In late 2005 a number of mala were reintroduced into a fenced enclosure in Uluru-Kata Tjuta National Park. Anangu Aboriginal elders celebrated their return. The last truly wild mala vanished after a wildfire swept through their habitat in the Tanami Desert in 1991, and there have been no recorded sightings since.

The Nyoongah name for the rufous hare wallaby is "wurrup".

The word "warla", a Warlpiri word, means "to depend on another for wellbeing".

An alternative spelling for mala told to Sophia while in the desert is marla.

Liliana Stafford